For Celine and Billie

www.hmhco.com

The text of this book is set in Garamond.
The illustrations are pastels on paper.

Library of Congress Cataloging-in-Publication Data
Mader, C. Roger, author, illustrator.
Tiptop cat / written and illustrated by C. Roger Mader.
pages cm
Summary: A cat finds the courage to climb again after a frightening fall
from his owner's apartment balcony.
ISBN 978-0-544-14799-7
1. Cats—Juvenile fiction. [1. Cats—Fiction.] I. Title.
PZ10.3.M25Ti 2014
[E]—dc23
2013038998

Manufactured in China
SCP 10 9 8 7 6 5 4 3 2 1
4500483629

TIPTOP
CAT

Written and illustrated by C. Roger Mader

HOUGHTON MIFFLIN HARCOURT
Boston   New York

Of all the gifts she got that day,
the best one was the cat.

The cat took a look around

and liked his new home.

He especially liked . . .

. . . the balcony.

From there he could get to . . .

. . . the rooftops!

In a short time he knew the neighborhood

And every day

like the back of his paw.

he would climb all the way up

to his favorite spot . . .

One day he heard the "coo, coo" of a pigeon

A little jungle beast

as she landed on *his* balcony.

awoke within the cat and said . . .

"POUNCE!"   So he pounced.

But cats can't fly, and he went . . .

. . . down . . .

. . . down . . .

. . . down . . .

. . . down!

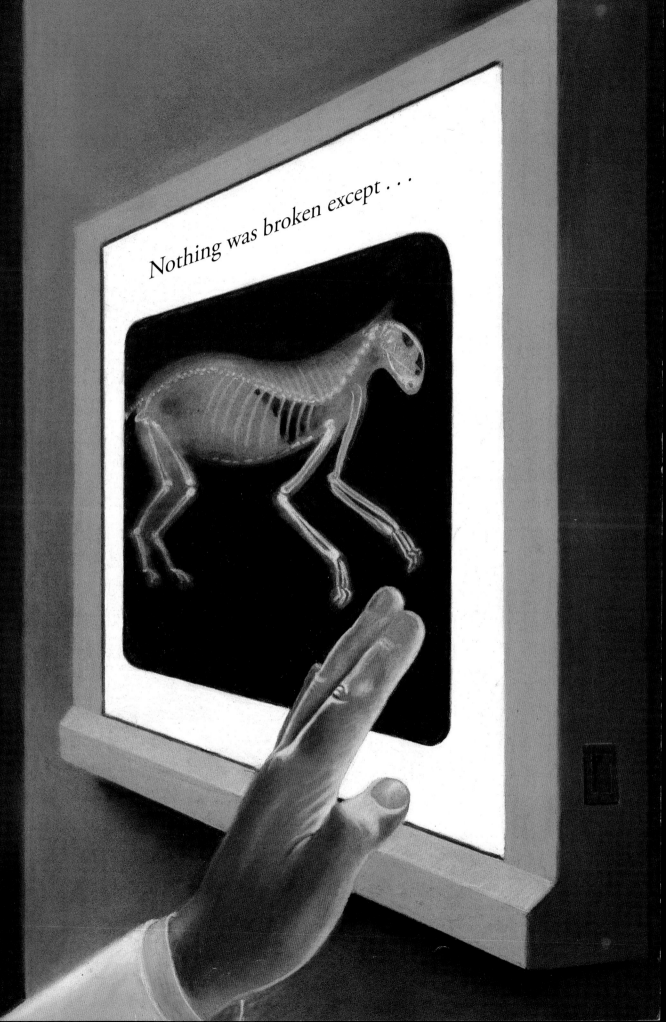

. . . his spirit!

No more balcony,

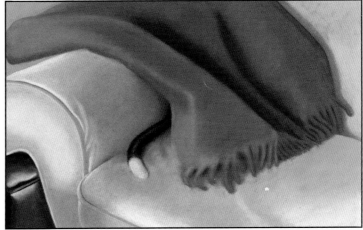

no more rooftops,

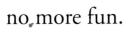
no more fun.

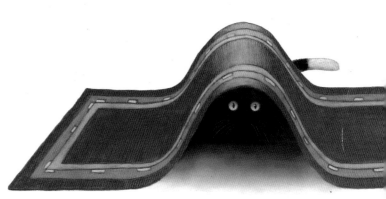

Until . . .

. . . and that inner beast stirred again.

The crow flew up . . .

. . . a crow showed up . . .

. . . the cat jumped up.

The crow went up . . .

. . . the cat went up . . .

. . . and up . . .

. . . and up . . .

. . . and up . . .

. . . and up . . .   . . . until he found himself . . .

. . . on top of the world again.